W9-CNL-511

# The Dragon Kite

ABOUT THE STORY.   The thief Ishikawa is a historical figure who lived in the late 1600s or early 1700s. There are several stories about his attempt to steal the golden dolphins that adorned the roof of Nagoya Castle. Ishikawa's motivation is not known; in this story he becomes the outlaw who steals from the rich to help the poor. This Robin Hood-type character is popular in Japanese tales. The dragon, who in this story thwarts the harsh verdict of history, was venerated as a supernatural being in Japan and China for centuries.

After Ishikawa's daring thievery, the Shogun forbade the construction of large kites, and iron cages were built around the dolphins. Later, however, someone else did manage to steal them.

Ishikawa's story is mentioned in several books about kites, including *Kites: A Historical Survey* by Clive Hart, *Art of the Japanese Kite* by Tal Streeter, and *The Complete Book of Kites and Kiteflying* by Will Yolen.

NANCY LUENN

The

HARCOURT BRACE & COMPANY   •   San Diego    New York    London

# Dragon Kite

## ILLUSTRATED BY MICHAEL HAGUE

FOR THAD CURTZ

Text copyright © 1982 by Nancy Luenn
Illustrations copyright © 1982 by Michael Hague

All rights reserved. No part of
this publication may be reproduced or
transmitted in any form or by any means,
electronic or mechanical, including photocopy,
recording, or any information storage and
retrieval system, without permission
in writing from the publisher.

Requests for permission to make copies of
any part of the work should be mailed to
Permissions Department
Harcourt Brace & Company,
8th Floor, Orlando, Florida 32887.

Printed and bound by
Impresora Donneco International, Mexico

Library Of Congress Cataloging-in-Publication Data
Luenn, Nancy.      The dragon kite.
SUMMARY: A crafty thief constructs a magnificent kite
which he hopes will enable him to reach the golden
dolphins that adorn the roof of a nearby castle.
1. Ishikawa, Goemon, d. 1594—Juvenile fiction.
[1. Ishikawa, Goemon, d. 1594—Fiction.
2. Kites—Fiction.   3. Robbers and outlaws—Fiction.
4. Japan—Fiction]   I. Hague, Michael, ill.   II. Title.
PZ7.L9766Dr      [E]      81-11709
ISBN 0-15-224197-3      AACR2
C D E F G

Printed in Mexico

*Grateful acknowledgment is made to Yasuko Shimizu,*
*whose antique family kimono was photographed for use as*
*the border pattern on the art throughout the book.*

WHEN THE SHOGUN was master of all Japan, there lived a thief named Ishikawa. He was different from most thieves. Ishikawa spent the gold he stole buying rice for hungry people in the villages and kept only enough to feed his small family. In gratitude, the villagers hid him from the Shogun's soldiers.

The Shogun built a magnificent castle for his son, and on its highest rooftop were a pair of golden dolphins. They seemed to swim along the wind with their tails saluting the sky. Ishikawa wanted to steal them.

"Imagine all the rice I could buy with that gold," he thought. "The Shogun's son has gold and silk to wear, and fish on his table. He does not need the statues." He often stood outside the castle staring up at the dolphins and asked the Cloud Dragon to show him a way. But try as he might, Ishikawa could not think of any way to steal them.

One day, as he stood near the castle, he watched a runaway kite dancing in the sky. It seemed to bow to the sun and beg the wind to send it higher into the blue. But the wind threw it hard against a dolphin and it crumpled, drifting down to lie at Ishikawa's feet. He stood still, angry at the wind and at the dolphin.

Then suddenly he smiled.

"Of course," he murmured. "I could use a kite. But it must be well crafted, or it and I will meet the fate of this one."

Ishikawa hurried home. He greeted his wife with a smile and swung his small son into the air.

"I am going to steal the golden *shachi*," he told his wife, Oritsu. "I will build a giant kite that will carry me to the highest rooftop. Think of all the rice that gold will buy!"

"This is madness," cried Oritsu. "We will die for your foolishness. Our deaths will not feed the people."

Ishikawa hardly listened. "I need someone to hold the kite reins," he thought. He set off to find three friends who had often helped him. He went to the house of Hayami the philosopher and found all three sitting in the garden.

"I am going to steal the golden *shachi* from the castle," said Ishikawa, "with the help of a giant kite. I need you to hold the reins for me. The gold from the statues will buy a thousand bags of rice!"

The three men stared at Ishikawa for a minute. Then Sentaro the goldsmith laughed and said, "But where will you find such a kite?"

"I will build it," replied Ishikawa impatiently.

"You do not have the skill of kitemakers," reasoned Hayami. "Accept what is, Ishikawa—the golden *shachi* are beyond the reach of men. Only the wisdom and strength of a dragon could touch them."

"Then it shall be a dragon kite," vowed Ishikawa, "and I will learn the kitemaker's art."

"How will you carry down the golden *shachi?*" Iwaki, the rice merchant, asked. "They must be very heavy."

"I will build a kite so beautiful and strong that the wind will bow down and carry it, no matter what the weight," replied Ishikawa.

The three men shook their heads sadly. Surely he had come to the end of wisdom.

Ishikawa was a stubborn man. In the morning he went to the shop of Katsuta. The kitemaker was an old man with eyes as patient as still water. He rose and bowed to Ishikawa.

"I know who you are," said Katsuta. "But your name is safe in my keeping."

"I wish to make kites," said Ishikawa.

Katsuta considered the proud young man. "You lack patience," he said.

"I will learn it," replied the thief.

"You do not know the ways of bamboo and paper," continued Katsuta.

"I will learn them."

"You have no skill with brush and paint," the kitemaker told him.

"This, too, I will learn."

The old man smiled and nodded slowly, for he was pleased with Ishikawa's determination.

Ishikawa hoped that he would soon hold a brush, but Katsuta said, "No. There are many things that you must learn first. A kitemaker must know when the bamboo is ready. He must be able to cut it clean and strong. He must know how to mix the paste that holds the kite's skin to its bones, and the colors that give it a name."

So Ishikawa cut bamboo and mixed paste and paint while restlessness ran round inside him like mice inside a wall. Bright colors splattered his kimono, and his fingers stuck together with paste. His hands ached from cutting the bamboo. But he would not give up.

All this time Katsuta made kites. Ishikawa watched while the old man painted a curling wave onto the strong kite paper. Katsuta tied the bamboo bones together and pasted the kite skin to its bones. Then he carefully tied the cords that would be the kite's bridle. The kitemaker took two lengths of cord to be its reins.

"The wind brings the kite alive," he told Ishikawa, "and the reins keep it tied to the earth. Without the reins a kite will fly to its death. Only the

greatest of kites, the dragons who touch the heavens, need no reins."

The thief worked through winter and into spring. When the swallows tumbled into the city on the wind, Ishikawa held the reins of a warrior kite. He felt it tug against his hands, and his heart soared with the swallows. He stole just enough to feed his wife and son. Oritsu was glad that her husband made kites, but she dreaded the day he would try to steal the golden dolphins.

"Be a kitemaker," she pleaded. "Do not try to steal the *shachi*." But her words were like fading cherry blossoms before the dolphins, which swam endlessly in the wind of his mind.

As the second year grew cold, Katsuta allowed the thief to lay the bones of his first kite. He pasted the skin to the bones and set it aside. The kites would wait until spring. In the winter days Ishikawa and Katsuta made lanterns to brighten the homes of the city. Ishikawa helped with many things now, but Katsuta always painted the designs. One day the thief could wait no longer.

"When will I hold a brush?" he asked.

"When the swallows return," replied the kitemaker calmly.

Ishikawa's heart sank, but he was silent. The dolphins seemed to mock him as they floated in the winter sky, too far away to ever be touched.

One windy day the swallows returned. Ishikawa touched a brush to paper, and swirls of paint filled its surface. He watched eagerly for the finished design, but the lines of paint did not go where he wished. His colors were as rippled as the windy sea, and his hand was clumsy. Ruined paintings piled up around him, but when Ishikawa's temper flared, the kitemaker looked at him silently. The young man bent his head and tried again. Slowly the skill began to come. He drew warriors' faces and leaping hares. But most of all he drew dragons, on every scrap of paper he could find. Soon he and Katsuta shared equally in the tasks, and finished kites filled every corner of the room.

Ishikawa worked for another year and more, learning all that Katsuta could teach him. On a day when the springtime wind called to kites, he

said to Katsuta, "I have worked for four years now, honored one. Give me leave to go."

The old man nodded, his eyes as quiet as a pool in shadow.

Ishikawa returned home, stopping first to buy bamboo and paper, and the powder for paints. Beneath a blossoming cherry tree he began to build the giant kite. The work was as joyful as water leaping down the mountains. He felt sure that this kite would touch the heavens.

When it was finished, he went to find his three friends.

"Come and see the kite I have made," said Ishikawa. "Then you will know that my plan is a good one!" The three men shook their heads doubtfully as they followed Ishikawa back to the garden.

They stood amazed. A red and silver dragon coiled across the garden, its mighty wings a royal purple. Its eyes were the color of an autumn pool, mirroring the eyes of Katsuta.

"It is a well-made kite," Hayami murmured. The others nodded. A sea wind eddied through the garden, and the dragon kite stirred impatiently.

"Tonight," said Ishikawa, "we will go to the plain near the castle. The kite will soar on the wind, and at last I will touch the golden *shachi*."

As they walked silently through the whispering spring night, the great kite moved restlessly in their hands. Iwaki held it steady while the thief climbed into the harness below the frame. The kite bowed under his weight and then rose into the sky. Hayami loosened the reins.

The wind captured the kite and lifted it higher. Ishikawa clung to the bamboo bones with taut hands. The trees fell away beneath him, and he could see the width of Nobi Plain. The wind carried him like the swift current of a river. Soon he looked down on the castle. Dark figures carried torches in the courtyard below, blind to the dragon that flew silently above them. The wind chuckled in Ishikawa's ear. Then the kite grazed against one of the statues. Ishikawa sighed and stepped down, fastening his kite to the dolphin's tail. He put his shoulder against the dolphin and tried to move it. The statue did not budge. He tried again and again without success, while the dolphin taunted him with its stillness. Finally

Ishikawa slumped down and thrust his chin onto his fists. The kite nudged him gently. Ishikawa looked up. The dark eyes of the dragon asked a silent question.

*What did you learn from making kites?*

"To try again," replied Ishikawa.

*What more?*

"Accept what is and try again," murmured the thief. He stood up and examined the dolphin. He grasped a fin and pulled. It came loose in his hand. He pulled off the other fin, then scrambled up the dolphin's tail to take the tail fins. Ishikawa crept along the roof to the other dolphin and stole its fins as well. He fastened them to the kite with strong cord. As he slashed the line that tethered the kite, he held his breath. What if the kite could not carry them?

Ishikawa grasped the kite firmly with both hands and walked to the edge of the roof. He put one foot on the ropes and asked the Cloud Dragon for courage. The blood sang in his ears as he jumped.

The kite drifted away from the roof and faltered, dropping toward the guarded castle walls. Ishikawa closed his eyes, and his stomach tightened. Then he felt the wind on his back like a dragon's breath. The kite rose slowly, humming the wild, sweet song of creatures with wings. The watching men hauled in the reins.

Ishikawa stepped down from the kite. The others crowded round him.

"I could not move the rest," he admitted, handing them the fins. "But this gold will buy a hundred bags of rice or more."

Sentaro's eyes shone at the sight of so much gold. "These were easily gained," he said, chuckling.

Ishikawa thought of the years in Katsuta's shop and turned to the kite. It tugged at the reins, the dragon's silver shining dimly in the night. He bowed low.

"Go free, great one. May the wind carry you high into the heavens." He cut the reins with his knife, and it seemed to him that the dragon smiled. The kite rose slowly into the night, perfectly balanced on the wind.

"The dragons have no need of the reins," murmured Ishikawa. The four men watched it disappear, then staggered into the darkness with their burden of gold.

They took the gold to Sentaro's shop to be melted down, and all seemed well. Two days later Ishikawa heard a pounding at his door.

"Sentaro has betrayed you," whispered Iwaki frantically. "Flee!"

It was too late. The thief's house was swarming with soldiers. He and his family were bound with rope and taken to the castle.

Ishikawa and his family were led into a large room. The Shogun's son sat frowning down on them. One of the soldiers bowed low and said, "Venerated lord, this man was the student of Katsuta the kitemaker."

"Bring Katsuta here," ordered the Shogun's son.

Now four prisoners knelt before the lord of the castle. The lord said, "Ishikawa, you are a thief. For thieving you shall die, and these three will die with you as a warning to other foolish folk. The boiling oil will greet you in the morning."

The Shogun's son stood up and stalked away. Soldiers led the prisoners to a small room. The door slammed shut. Oritsu turned her face to the wall and began to weep.

"I did not think," said Ishikawa sadly to the kitemaker, "that harm would come to you. I thought only of gaining the *shachi,* and I did not think of what might happen to my friends and family." He put his hand on Oritsu's shoulder.

"It is done," said Katsuta. "It is a great deed to build such a kite."

When morning came, they were led into a courtyard. A huge metal tub stood below a wooden platform. Flames leaped around it. Soldiers flanked the prisoners as they climbed onto the platform.

"Execute them," commanded the Shogun's son.

As the soldiers moved to obey, a giant shadow crossed the sun. The prisoners were lifted in the claws of a red and silver dragon. Swift arrows glanced harmlessly off his scales. His lashing tail upset the boiling oil, and the soldiers ran for their lives.

As the prisoners were carried into the gentle blue sky, they heard the sweet, hissing voice of the dragon.

"Greetings to you, Ishikawa. The lord of the castle is angry because you have stolen his gold. He says that you should die. But I say that he who gives freedom should live, and you cut the reins of the kite that I was."

The dragon flew west above Japan. Rice fields gave way to deep forests as they glided over the mountains. The wind sang a wild, shrill song as it whistled along the dragon's wings. They saw the gilded roofs of the Emperor's palace beside the shores of Lake Biwa. People in the fields fell to the ground as the dragon passed overhead. But he flew on, across the Inland Sea. At last they came to a city built on hills above the ocean. The dragon glided down into a field outside the city.

"The Shogun's son will not trouble you here," he told them, "and the city has need of kitemakers." The dragon paused, regarding Ishikawa with eyes like a pool in shadow. "Be a kitemaker, Ishikawa, and my blessing will go with you, for I was once a well-made kite."

0594